D1119986

IMAGINE

WRITTEN AND ILLUSTRATED BY BART VIVIAN

ALADDIN

New York London Toronto Sydney New Delhi

BEYONDWORDS

Hillsboro, Oregon

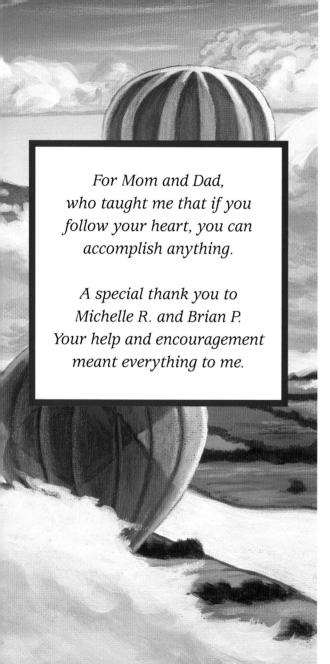

*For Mom and Dad,
who taught me that if you
follow your heart, you can
accomplish anything.*

*A special thank you to
Michelle R. and Brian P.
Your help and encouragement
meant everything to me.*

ALADDIN
An imprint of Simon & Schuster
Children's Publishing Division
1230 Avenue of the Americas
New York, NY 10020

BEYOND WORDS
20827 N.W. Cornell Road, Suite 500
Hillsboro, Oregon 97124-9808
503-531-8700 / 503-531-8773 fax
www.beyondword.com

This Aladdin/Beyond Words hardcover edition April 2013
Copyright text and illustrations © 1998 by Bart Vivian

For information about special discounts for bulk purchases, please contact Simon & Schuster Special Sales at 1-866-506-1949 or business@simonandschuster.com.

The Simon & Schuster Speakers Bureau can bring authors to your live event.
For more information or to book an event contact the Simon & Schuster Speakers Bureau at 1-866-248-3049 or visit our website at www.simonspeakers.com.

Editor: Michelle Roehm McCann
Design: DesignWise, Sara E. Blum
The text of this book was set in ITC Usherwood.
The illustrations for this book were rendered in Adobe Photoshop.

Manufactured in China 0213 SCP

10 9 8 7 6 5 4 3 2 1

Library of Congress Cataloging-in-Publication Data

Vivian, Bart.
   Imagine / written and illustrated by Bart Vivian.
      p.   cm.
   Summary: Asks readers to imagine ordinary, everyday events as wondrous and
      magical occurrences.
   [1. Imagination—Fiction.] I. Title.
PZ7.V8285Im 2013
[E]—dc23
                                                              2012012467

ISBN: 978-1-58270-329-9
ISBN: 978-1-4422-4546-8 (ebook)

If you can imagine things aren't quite what they seem, and dream of possibilities that only you can dream of, then *anything* can happen.

Imagine that your tree house . . .

...is more than
just a tree house.

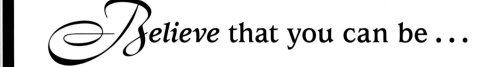

Believe that you can be . . .

...whatever your heart desires.

magine that one day . . .

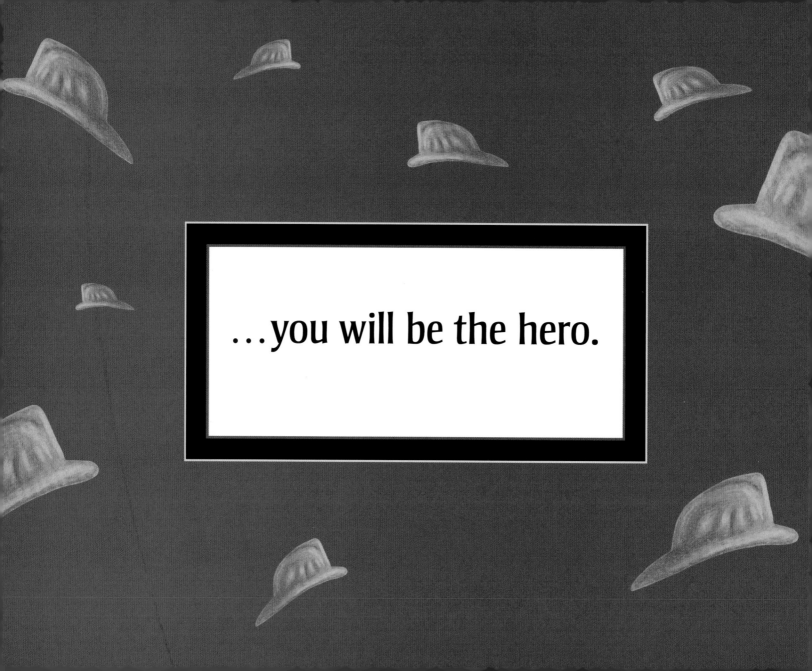

…you will be the hero.

$\mathcal{D}$*ream* of adventures . . .

...that are just beyond the horizon.

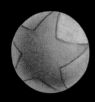

B*elieve* that no fear ...

...is too BiG to face.

magine voyages . . .

...across oceans you've never seen.

$\mathcal{B}$*elieve* that you can overcome ...

...all obstacles in your path.

Imagine the possibilities that await you...it's all just a dream away.